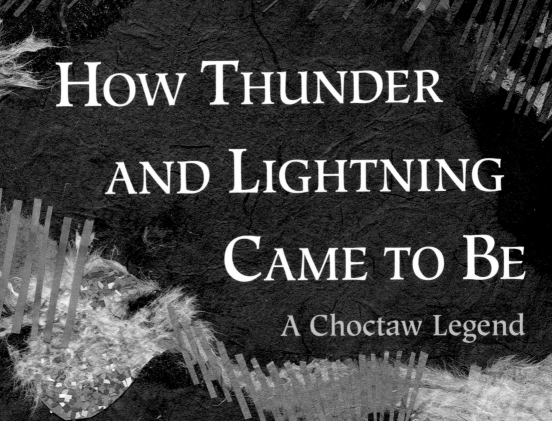

HOW THUNDER
AND LIGHTNING
CAME TO BE

A Choctaw Legend

retold by BEATRICE ORCUTT HARRELL

collages by SUSAN L. ROTH

Dial Books for Young Readers
New York

*For my husband, Robert; for Len Green, who spoke to me
from the spirit world; for the Orcutt tribe and my own little tribe;
and most of all for my people, the Choctaw*

B.O.H.

For Jesse, with love

S.L.R.

I would like to thank Ann Finnell, Alex Roth, and the following people from
the Museum of Natural History, Smithsonian Institution: Mayda Riopedre
(Anthropology Library) and Neil Hauck, Vyrtis Thomas, and Cathy Creek
(National Anthropological Archives). All of them ably assisted me. — S.L.R.

Published by Dial Books for Young Readers
A Division of Penguin Books USA Inc.
375 Hudson Street
New York, New York 10014

Text copyright © 1995 by Beatrice Orcutt Harrell
Pictures copyright © 1995 by Susan L. Roth
All rights reserved
Designed by Ann Finnell
Printed in Hong Kong
First Edition
1 3 5 7 9 10 8 6 4 2

Library of Congress Cataloging in Publication Data
Harrell, Beatrice Orcutt.
How thunder and lightning came to be: a Choctaw legend/retold by Beatrice Orcutt Harrell;
collages by Susan L. Roth.—1st ed.
p. cm.
Summary: Two very large and silly birds accidentally create thunder and
lightning as a way to warn the Choctaw people of coming rainstorms.
ISBN 0-8037-1748-2 (trade).—ISBN 0-8037-1749-0 (library)
1. Choctaw Indians—Folklore. 2. Legends—Southern States. 3. Thunder—Folklore.
4. Lightning—Folklore. [1. Choctaw Indians—Folklore. 2. Indians of North
America—Folklore. 3. Folklore—Southern States. 4. Thunder—Folklore.
5. Lightning—Folklore. 6. Thunderstorms—Folklore.]
I. Roth, Susan L., ill. II. Title.
E99.C8H295 1995 398.2'089973—dc20 [E] 94-17457 CIP AC

I painted this book with paper. My big scissors are my big brushes; my little scissors are
my little brushes; and tweezers thin as needles are my one-haired brushes. Japanese
glue, or *nori*, is my linseed oil, and my papers, collected by me from everywhere in
the world, are both my canvas and my paint. — S.L.R.

AUTHOR'S NOTE

In the old language they called themselves Okla, which means The People. Sometime after the European invasion the name of The People was anglicized to Chata and Chata became Choctaw. This ancient tribe of people lived for thousands of years on land that is now called Mississippi, Alabama, and Georgia. The People lived in a world filled with mystery and magic. Spirits, imps, animal people, and Hashtahli, The Great Sun Father, were woven into the fabric of their everyday lives. Stories that explained the origin of humans, animals, and natural events were filled with these beings. These tales were passed down from generation to generation via the oral tradition.

My mother, Juanita Walker Orcutt, was a full-blood Choctaw, and from her I knew that thunder and lightning were only two great birds who lived on the clouds, and that I had nothing to fear from them. My aunt, Myrtle Walker, and my grandfather, Clayton Ishcomer, told me the same legend, with more varied and descriptive detail. This retelling is a combination of all three of those versions, and my own efforts to make Melatha's silly warnings both vivid and true to the ancient Choctaw ways.

This particular story is mentioned briefly in *Source Material for the Social and Ceremonial Life of the Choctaw* by John R. Swanton, Bureau of American Ethnology Bulletin 103, p. 212; but my only purpose in citing this source is to stress that there is documentation of the tale's authenticity, independently of the oral tradition. Such is not always the case.

In the time of long ago, The Great Sun Father wanted to give his chosen people, the Choctaw, a warning to seek shelter before he sent the wind and rain to the earth.

He thought for many days, but he could not decide what the best warning would be. Since he was busy with other things, he thought he would get someone else to work on the problem.

He called on two great, silly birds who had nothing else to do. "I will give you a home on top of the clouds," he said, "if you will think of a good way to warn my chosen people of any coming storms."

Heloha and Melatha were proud and happy to be called upon to help The Great Sun Father. Heloha was big and slow-moving, while her mate, Melatha, was much smaller and very, very fast. He was also very clumsy.

Once the two birds were settled in their new home, they began to think about ways to warn the people. This was not going to be easy, because they were not the smartest of birds.

"Melatha, my husband, I have an idea," Heloha said. "Could you stick your head down through the clouds and shout very loudly that a storm is coming?"

Melatha thought about this for a while, then nodded his head. "That is a good idea, my dear. Let us see if it will work."

So Melatha stuck his head into the clouds, but he could not see anything. He leaned over a little farther, but still he could not see anything, so he leaned over even farther.

His feet flew out from under him, and he fell out of the clouds and went tumbling to earth.

Melatha landed right in the middle of a Choctaw cornfield, and a big dust cloud rose all around him. He jumped up and began to try to brush the dirt off his feathers.

The children of the village were picking ripe corn when Melatha fell out of the sky. They stared at the huge, dusty bird and did not know whether to laugh or run away. Feeling very silly, Melatha began to flap his wings to get the dust off.

As he flapped those big wings, the dust cloud grew bigger and bigger, and then he started to sneeze. Achoo! Achoo! Achoo! As he rose into the air, he continued to sneeze. Achoo! Achoo! The children laughed and shouted as Melatha and the dust cloud went higher and higher into the sky, until the sound of sneezing finally faded away.

When he was home again, Heloha fussed over him and gave him cold water to drink. "I'm sorry, my husband, for giving you such a bad idea," she said.

"No, no, my lovely Heloha. It was a good idea, but I am too clumsy. Come, let us think of something else," Melatha said.

The next day Melatha had a new idea. "I will go down to the earth and run from village to village, calling out a warning as I pass. I will have to run my fastest to get to everyone in time, but I am sure this plan will work. What do you think, Heloha?"

"I think it is a fine idea, my dear, and well worth a try," Heloha answered.

The Choctaw villages were scattered across many miles of hills, swamps, and forests, and Melatha called upon all of his great speed to reach each one.

"A storm is coming. A storm is coming," he shouted. But he was moving so fast that his words were lost in the wind. The people watched in silent amazement as Melatha flashed by and disappeared in a swirl of dust and autumn leaves.

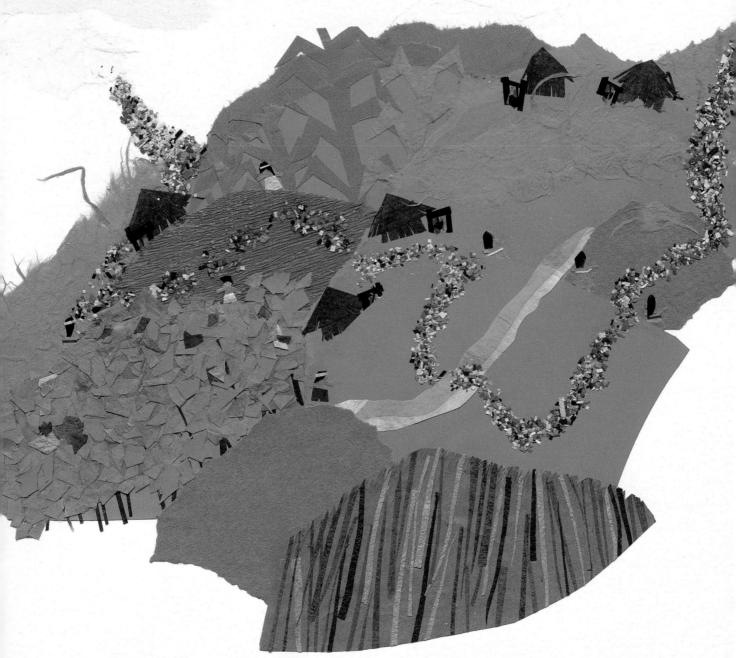

On he raced, moving faster than any whirlwind. Around the swamps and through the forests he sped, thinking only of the need to hurry—when suddenly, Splash! He fell right into a stream that ran, laughing and singing, along the forest floor. The cold water soaked his feathers and chilled his feet before he could climb onto dry earth again.

Dripping and shivering, he made his way home to Heloha. "You did the best you could, my love," she said, "and that is all anyone can do. We will work on this another time."

But the next day it was time for Heloha to lay her eggs. The clouds in her new home were so soft and fluffy, she decided to lay her eggs there instead of building a nest.

As soon as Heloha laid the giant eggs, they began to roll. "Melatha, my husband, could you come and catch the eggs, please?" She called loudly, for Melatha was fond of roaming far from home.

Melatha was indeed far from home, but he heard his wife calling him. "I'm coming, my dear. I'll be right there," he shouted back. He called on every bit of his great speed, and ran flashing across the sky with sparks flying from his heels.

He ran so fast that his feet got tangled up, and he fell out of the clouds and hit a tree on the earth.

The sparks flew, crackling and popping, and the tree split in half, but the Choctaw people hardly noticed because they were having a noisy celebration. It was the time of the Green Corn dance, when the people gave thanks to The Great Sun Father for their good harvest.

A big drum, played by two drummers, sat in the center of the village, and around it the people were singing and dancing. The children were playing chase with the dogs, wrestling with one another, and dancing their own little dances.

When Melatha hit the tree, he sat back on his tail feathers and felt a little dizzy, but he jumped up and flew back into the clouds.

This time some of the children looked up, and they remembered him. They laughed and clapped as he streaked across the sky, but Melatha was moving too fast to notice.

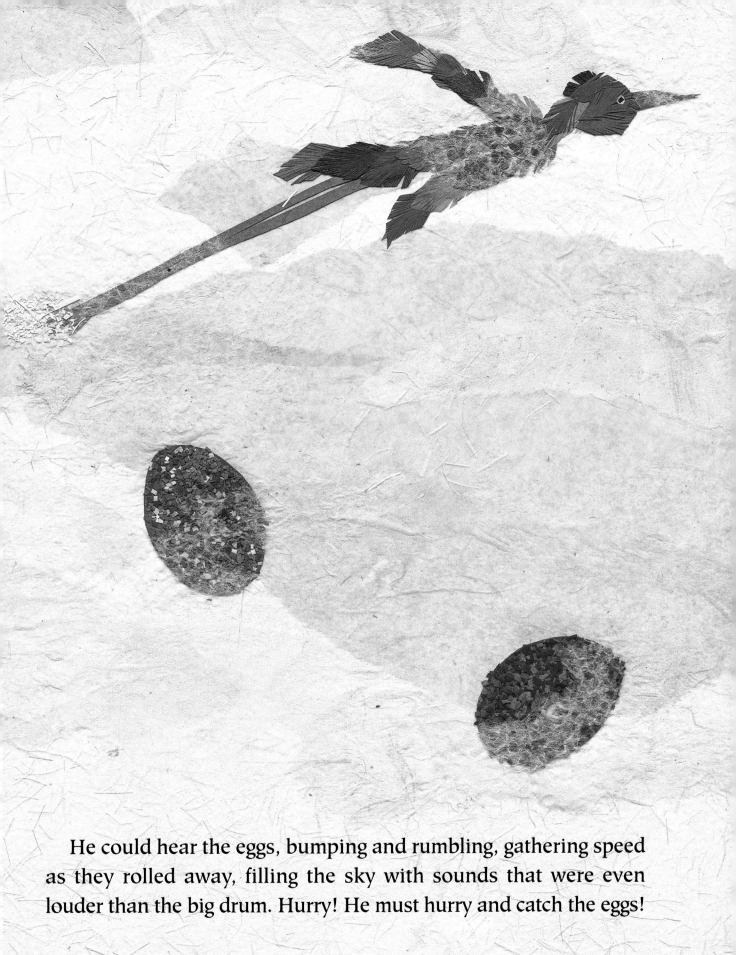

He could hear the eggs, bumping and rumbling, gathering speed as they rolled away, filling the sky with sounds that were even louder than the big drum. Hurry! He must hurry and catch the eggs!

But he was too late. The eggs rolled faster and faster across the endless clouds until they were lost.

Melatha went to tell his wife the bad news. "I didn't catch the eggs because I am clumsy and foolish," he said sadly.

"Melatha, my love, do not worry. We have plenty of time, and there will be other eggs. You are safe and we are together, so all is well." Heloha smiled and Melatha was happy again.

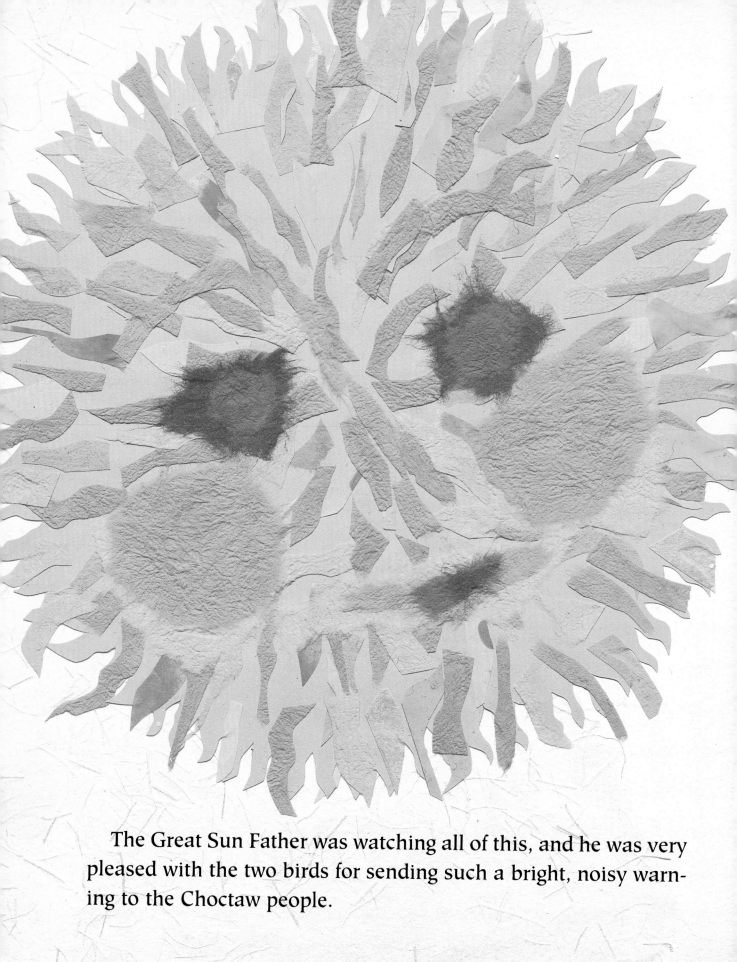

The Great Sun Father was watching all of this, and he was very pleased with the two birds for sending such a bright, noisy warning to the Choctaw people.

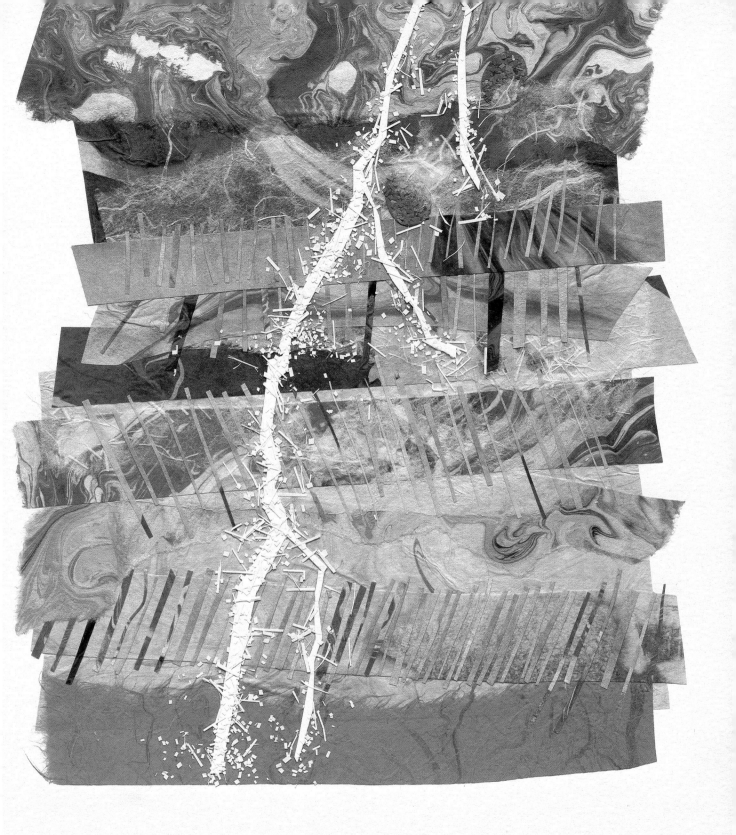

From that time to this, whenever Heloha lays her eggs and Melatha chases them, The Great Sun Father calls the wind and sends the rain falling to the earth.

Heloha continues to lay her eggs on the clouds. She does not worry, for she knows that one day her swift Melatha will catch enough to make a fine little family.

In time Melatha's name came to mean lightning and Heloha's thunder, and they are still trying to think of a good warning to send the Choctaw people when a storm is coming.